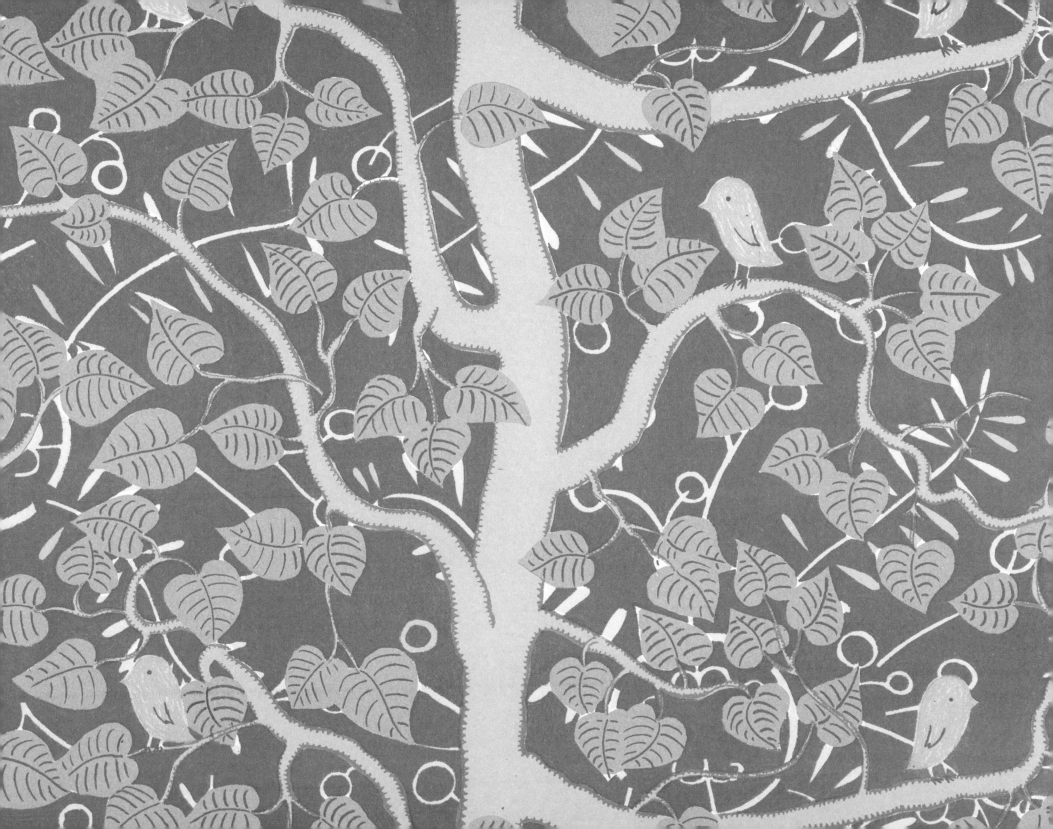

For Joseph

First published in 2016 by Child's Play (International) Ltd
Ashworth Road, Bridgemead, Swindon SN5 7YD, UK

Published in USA by Child's Play Inc
250 Minot Avenue, Auburn, Maine 04210

Distributed in Australia by Child's Play Australia Pty Ltd
Unit 10/20 Narabang Way, Belrose, Sydney, NSW 2085

ISBN 978-1-84643-694-9
L120615CPL01166949

Printed in Heshan, China

1 3 5 7 9 10 8 6 4 2

A catalogue record of this book
is available from the British Library

www.childs-play.com

MR MOON

wakes up

JEMIMA SHARPE

Mr Moon always sleeps.

He naps during hide-and-seek,

passes out on puzzles,

dozes during adventure stories,

and never makes polite
conversation at tea parties.

He is a very good
bedtime companion.

Sometimes I wish he were a bit more exciting.
Maybe he doesn't like games or books or tea.

Hey! You're awake! Where are you going?

I don't remember those birds singing before.

How did you get
in there, Mr Moon?

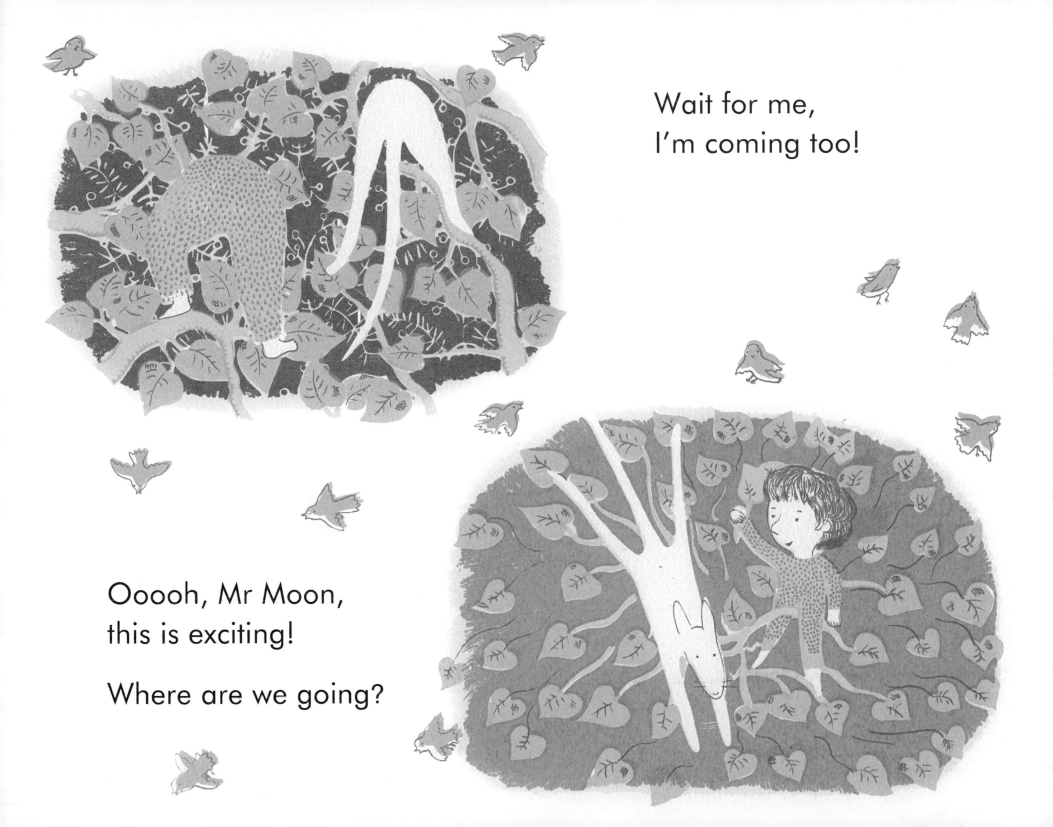

Wait for me,
I'm coming too!

Ooooh, Mr Moon,
this is exciting!

Where are we going?

Mr Moon is good at making friends.

Get ready to run, Mr Moon!

Mr Moon does like games after all!

Mr Moon can solve really big puzzles.

Let's race to
the middle again!

He loves books about adventures...

and messing about in boats.

Please may I have a go
with the oars, Mr Moon?

What Mr Moon likes most of all...

is a good
TEA PARTY!

I feel a little bit sleepy now.

Goodnight, garden.
Goodnight, everyone.

I'd like to go to bed.

Goodnight, Mr Moon.

Mr Moon?

Mr Moon always sleeps. Well, nearly always!

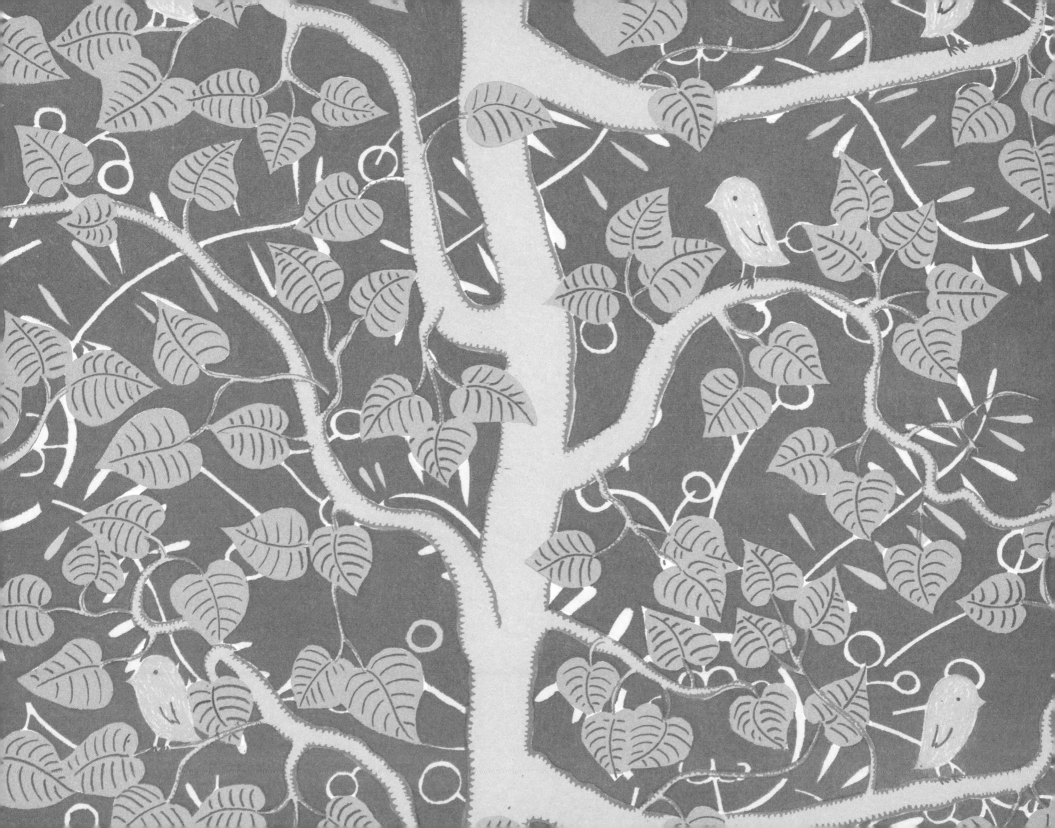